D0962635

Look for these
ROTTEN SCHOOL
books, too!

The Big
Blueberry
Barf~Off!

The Great
Smelling Bee

The Good,
the Bad and
the Very Slimy

Lose, Team, Lose!

Shake, Rattle,
& Hurl!

ROTTEN SCHOOL

The Heinie Prize

R.L. STINE

Illustrations by Trip Park

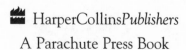

HarperCollins*Publishers*

A Parachute Press Book

For Mom
–TP

The Heinie Prize
Copyright © 2006 by Parachute Publishing, L.L.C.
Cover copyright © 2006 by Parachute Publishing, L.L.C.

For information address HarperCollins Children's Books, a division of HarperCollins
Publishers, 1350 Avenue of the Americas, New York, NY 10019.
www.harperchildrens.com

Library of Congress Cataloging-in-Publication Data
Stine, R.L.
   The Heinie Prize / R.L. Stine ; illustrations by Trip Park.— 1st ed.
      p.   cm. — (Rotten School ; 6)
   Summary: When fourth-grader Bernie schemes to have his servile friend Belzer win
the Most Outstanding Student award, his success yields unexpected consequences.
   ISBN-10: 0-06-078814-3 (trade bdg.) — ISBN-10: 0-06-078815-1 (lib. bdg.)
   ISBN-13: 978-0-06-078814-8 (trade bdg.) — ISBN-13: 978-0-06-078815-5 (lib. bdg.)
   [1. Boarding schools—Fiction. 2. Schools—Fiction. 3. Awards—Fiction.
4. Behavior—Fiction.] I. Park, Trip, ill. II. Title. III. Series.
PZ7.S86037Hei 2006   2005037031
[Fic]—dc22   CIP
                                                                              AC

Cover and interior design by mjcdesign
1 2 3 4 5 6 7 8 9 10

First Edition

——:CONTENTS:——

Morning Announcements 1

1. Foam Fight! 3

2. Who Will Win the Heinie? 8

3. "Dream On ..." 12

4. A Surprising Letter 17

5. Belzer Is Outta There! 23

6. Belzer Is the MAN! 27

7. A High Fever? 31

8. A Flesh-Eating Disease 35

9. Bernie the Slave 37

10. Mrs. H. Has a Good Laugh 43

11. Why the Twins Screamed 50

12. A Bowling Accident 56

13. Nose Wars 62

14. Brilliant! 65

15. The Bernie Shuffle 68

16. "We Weren't Cheating!" 72

17. Moonlight Over Pooper's Pond 77

18. Belzer the Hero 82

19. A Surprise Winner 84

20. The King Speaks 90

21. The Monster Strikes! 95

22. A Palace for the King 101

23. King Belzer Suffers 103

24. 11:59 108

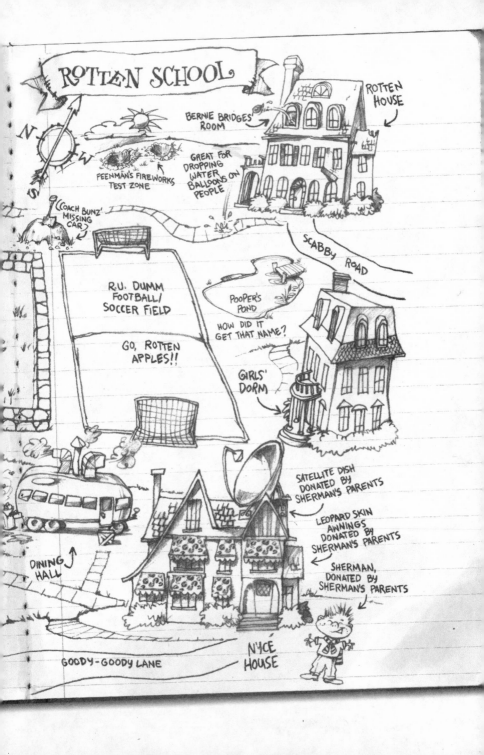

MORNING ANNOUNCEMENTS

Is this on? Can anyone hear me? Is this on? Good morning, Rotten Students. This is Headmaster Upchuck with today's Morning Announcements.

 Buck Naykid, president of the Fifth Grade Losers Club, announces the club has changed its name because so many kids made fun of it. The club's new name is The Maggots.

A special treat in the Dining Hall tonight. Chef

Baloney promises that the chickens will be plucked before they are served.

Nurse Hanley would like to remind all first graders that snot is not part of a healthy breakfast.

While we are on that subject . . . I know many of you were looking forward to the Sixth Grade Long-Distance Sneezing Contest. But it has been canceled because two contestants came down with colds.

Mr. Farrhowt, our music teacher, has canceled the Student All-Mozart Violin Concert for tonight since no one knows how to play the violin.

Finally, I'd like to warn everyone . . . fourth grade comedian, Harry Aip, will be showing off the chewed-up spinach in his teeth in the Dining Hall tonight. As long as you keep laughing at this, he'll keep doing it.

Chapter 1

FOAM FIGHT!

It was a hot, sunny day. The green grass gleamed under a clear blue sky. Birds twittered in the rotten apple trees.

My pals Feenman and Crench were walking across the Great Lawn with me. We had our cans of Foamy Root Beer raised high. And we were toasting one another and singing the Official Rotten School Song:

> *"Rah rah Rotten School!*
> *I'd rather be in Rotten School—*
> *Than NOT in school!"*

I have to admit it. Those tender words always bring tears to my eyes.

I'm Bernie Bridges, and I love my Rotten School. You probably go home every day after school. But our school is a boarding school, and we live here.

Why do I love it so much?

If *only* I weren't so modest, I'd tell you that I'm the KING here! I'd tell you that it's my PURE GENIUS that makes me the king.

Maybe you've heard other people say this about me. Of course, I'd *never* say it about myself.

"Rah rah Rotten School!"

We sang and slapped our root beer cans together. Feenman, Crench, and I love Foamy Root Beer. You know their slogan—"It's So Foamy, It Stays on Your Face for Hours!"

We tilted the cans to our mouths and took long drinks. Then we wiped the foam off our faces and did the Official Rotten School Burp.

Feenman holds the school record for the Three-Minute Burp. Is he proud of it? Does a weasel have feathers?

Crench is a talented burpsman, too. Every time

our teacher, Mrs. Heinie, turns her back, Crench lets out loud, disgusting belches—until the instant she turns around again.

So far, she hasn't caught him once.

Hey, my guys are *talented*!

"Rah rah Rotten School!"

I turned and saw that Feenman had a devilish look on his face. He shook his root beer can and sprayed foam down the front of Crench's school vest.

"Hey! Why'd you do that?" Crench screamed.

Feenman shrugged. "No reason."

Crench shook his soda can and shot a spray at Feenman. But Feenman ducked, and I got a Foamy Root Beer shower.

"Whoa—!" I shook my soda and let Crench have it in the face.

In a few seconds all three of us were *soaked*. We were wrestling on the ground, licking the foam off one another.

"Dudes! Stop!" I shouted, wiping root beer foam from my hair.

I saw my archenemy walking toward us. That

spoiled, rich kid, Sherman Oaks. And what was that shiny thing he was carrying?

I jumped to my feet and hurried over to check it out.

And that's when all the fuss about the Heinie Prize began.

Chapter 2

WHO WILL WIN THE HEINIE?

Sherman Oaks is tall and blond, has crinkly, blue eyes, and a stuck-up expression. Some guys told me he has a heart tattoo on his butt with the words I'M RICH.

But we don't know for sure. He doesn't shower with the rest of us after gym class. He pays a kid to shower for him.

I wiped foam off my face. My hair was sticky from the root beer, and my sneakers squished as I walked.

"What's Sherman carrying?" Crench asked.

"Looks like some kind of display case from a store," I said.

"You think he's gonna put his *money* on display?" Feenman asked.

"Hey, dudes," Sherman greeted us with a smile. He held the glass case in front of him with both hands.

"What's that?" I asked, pointing.

"It's a solid platinum display case," he said. "My parents paid two thousand dollars for it. They buy me anything I want because they want me to like them."

"But—what's it for?" I asked.

Sherman grinned. I had to shield my eyes from the bright glow of his teeth. "It's to display the Heinie Prize when I win it," he said.

I stared at Feenman and Crench. "Huh? The Heinie Prize?"

Sherman nodded. "Mrs. Heinie awards a silver trophy every year to the Most Outstanding Fourth Grader."

"Sherman, you'd better give me the case," I said. "Mrs. Heinie is crazy about me! I've probably already won."

Sherman tilted his perfect nose in the air and sneered at me. "Bernie," he said, "she doesn't award

the Heinie Prize for being soaked in root beer. To win, you have to be both an outstanding *student* and an outstanding *citizen*."

Feenman opened his mouth and let out a long Rotten School Burp.

"That was outstanding!" Crench said.

Sherman tilted his nose higher and sneered some more. "When I win the Heinie," he said, "I'm going to display it in the front hall of the Student Center so everyone will be reminded that I'm not just filthy rich—I'm also fabulous!"

Sherman walked away, humming to himself.

My whole body started to shake. I started to pant like a dog. My teeth rattled. My lips flopped up and down.

Feenman grabbed me by the shoulders. "Bernie— what's wrong?" he cried.

"I . . . I've gotta win that prize," I finally choked out. "I can't let Sherman Oaks win. I've gotta win the Heinie. I've gotta be Most Outstanding."

Feenman and Crench stared at me. "But—how?" they cried.

Chapter 3

"DREAM ON..."

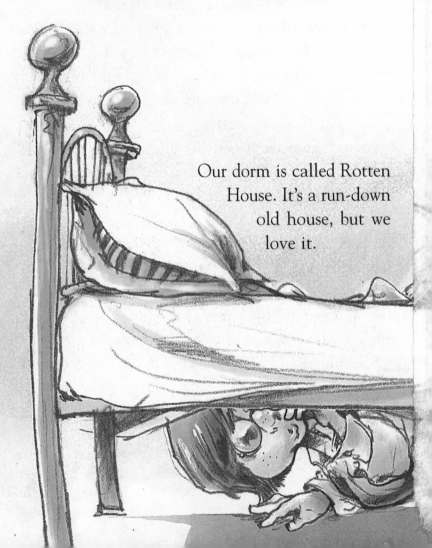

Our dorm is called Rotten House. It's a run-down old house, but we love it.

My buddies and I chose the third floor. It's perfect for dropping water balloons out the window when kids walk by.

Anything for a laugh—right?

That's *not* Mrs. Heinie's slogan. She is our dorm mother, so she has to be serious. She spends her time snooping and spying on us, making sure we *don't* do anything for a laugh.

I climbed the creaky stairs to my room and found Mrs. H. stretched out on the floor beside my bed. "Mrs. Heinie? Are you okay?" I cried.

She rolled over to face me. "I'm doing an under-the-bed inspection in every room," she said. "You'd be surprised at the things I find under beds."

"Really? Like what?"

"Well, on the second floor, I found a *boy* under his bed. He'd been there for three days."

"That's my friend Chipmunk," I said. "You know how shy he is. He doesn't like to come out."

She rolled over and pulled out a carton from under my bed. Inside was my secret stash of Nutty Nutty candy bars. I planned to sell them to the second graders for a dollar each.

"Aha!" she cried. "What have we here? Trying to hide something from me?"

"Yes," I said. "I am." I grabbed the carton from her hands. "Please, Mrs. H.—it's your birthday present. Please don't spoil the surprise."

She squinted at me through her thick eyeglasses. "My birthday present?" She shook the box. "Sounds like candy bars to me," she said.

She has an *awesome* ear!

I slid the box back under the bed. Then I helped her to her feet. "It's actually a *thank-you* present," I said. I flashed her my best, dimpled smile. The dimples in my cheeks always KILL!

"Thank you?" she said. "For what?"

I kept the awesome smile aimed at her. "I know I'm going to win the Heinie Prize," I said. "I just want to tell you how honored I am."

"You're joking, right?" she replied. She started for the door.

"No, wait. I want to show you something," I said. I pulled her to the window. "See this windowsill, Mrs. H.? That's where the prize trophy will go."

She rolled her eyes. "Dream on."

"Do you think you could lend the Heinie trophy to me now?" I asked. "I want to get used to having it in my room."

She stuck her finger down her throat and made a gagging sound.

"Is that a hint?" I said. "Are you trying to tell me I really *am* number one?"

"Bye, Bernie." She lumbered from the room, shaking her head.

I patted the windowsill. I pictured the silver trophy glowing in the sunlight with my name engraved on the front. Maybe one day I'd invite Sherman Oaks up for a quick glance at it.

"Yo, Big B!" A voice interrupted my daydream.

I spun around. "Belzer—what do you want?" I asked.

Chapter 4

A SURPRISING LETTER

"I finished your homework, Bernie," Belzer said. He set a stack of workbooks and binders down on my desk.

Belzer does my homework for me every night. He's a good kid. He knows I need time to plot and scheme for my guys here in Rotten House. *No way* I can fit homework into my busy schedule.

Belzer is a chubby, dumpy, schlumpy guy with floppy, red hair and a face full of freckles. He flashed me a crooked smile.

"I fed your parrot," Belzer said.

I turned to smile at Lippy, my beautiful green and red parrot, on his perch beside my bed.

"I'll beak your eye out!" he squawked.

"I'll beak you black and blue!"

"Ha-ha!" I laughed. "Isn't he cute? Who taught him to say those adorable things? Was it me?"

"Beak me!" Lippy cried.

"Bite rocks! Bite rocks and die!"

I shook my head. "He is the sweetest bird," I said. "Belzer, did you walk my dog?"

My fat bulldog, Gassy, was sprawled on my bed, snoring away as usual.

"Yes, I gave him a good walk," Belzer said. "You know, he has bad stomach problems. He stinks, Bernie. He really stinks."

"Always walk in front of him," I said. "Don't ever walk *behind* him." I glanced toward my closet. "Hey, my laundry bag is full," I said. "Guess I'll go do my laundry."

Belzer blocked my path. "No, please, Big B," he said. "You know how much I *love* doing your laundry. Please—let *me* do it!"

"Well…if you insist," I said. I shoved the bulging laundry bag into his arms.

Belzer is a good kid. It took a long time to train him. But it was worth it.

"Don't starch the shirts," I said. "I want everything soft. *Soft!*"

"You got it," Belzer said. He staggered to the door.

And Feenman stepped into the doorway. "You got a letter, Belzer," Feenman said.

Belzer reached for the envelope and dropped the laundry bag on Feenman's foot. Feenman stumbled over it and fell to the floor. Gassy lowered his head from the bed and started to lick Feenman's hair.

"Bite rocks! Bite rocks!"

Lippy squawked.

Belzer studied the envelope, moving his lips as he read. "Weird!" he said. "It's from my parents!"

Belzer's parents never write to him. The only letters he ever gets are from The Bald Man's Hair Club. No one knows *how* he got on their mailing list.

"Go ahead. Open it up," I said. "It might be important."

"Maybe they sent me money!" Belzer said.

"If they did," I replied, "you can pay me what you owe me for letting you do my laundry."

Belzer started to tear open the envelope. Little did I know that the letter would change my life FOREVER!

Chapter 5

BELZER IS OUTTA THERE!

Belzer held the letter close to his face and started to read it out loud. "'Dear Belzer,'" it began.

Even his parents call him Belzer! I don't think *anyone* knows his first name.

Dear Belzer,

All we hear from you is about this kid Bernie Bridges. Bernie this and Bernie that. It seems you have nothing else to write about.

You haven't accomplished anything at school. You seem to be a loser in every way.

We want to be proud of you. We don't want to be proud of someone named Bernie.

So, we are taking you out of Rotten School. We will send you to a school where you can amount to something.

Love,
Mom & Dad

Feenman and I stared in shock at Belzer. Belzer had his eyes on the letter. He was reading it again.

Finally, he turned to us with a sad sigh. "I have to go to another school," he muttered. "Guess I should start packing."

"Whoa! Hold it! Hold it!" I cried. I rushed across the room and grabbed Belzer by his flabby shoulders. "You're not leaving Rotten School just because your parents say so—*are* you?"

Belzer shrugged. "Yeah. I think so."

"Bad attitude!" I said. "You know Bernie B.'s motto—'Never Give Up!'"

"But, Bernie—" Belzer started to protest.

"Did I give up when Coach Bunz ordered us to climb the peaks of Mount Droolmann?" I asked.

24

"Bernie, that was a tiny hill," Feenman said. "And Belzer *carried* you to the top—remember?"

"Did I give up when Chef Baloney refused to give us second helpings of his famous mushroom chocolate chip ice cream? Did I give up when Mrs. Heinie insisted that Foamy Root Beer is not part of a healthy breakfast?"

I gave Belzer a hard slap on the back. "No!" I declared. "No! I never give up!"

Belzer let out a soft whimper. "But, Bernie—my parents say I have to leave."

"Don't worry about it," I said. "You're not going anywhere. Now, get outta here. Go do the laundry." I tossed him the bag and shoved him out the door.

I waited until Belzer had disappeared down the stairs. Then I turned to Feenman. I punched my fist into my hand. "They can't *do* this to me!" I shouted. "It took me *months* to train him! I don't want to lose such a good slave! Oops. I mean, such a good *friend*."

Feenman shook his head. "Belzer is a good guy," he said. "But what can you do?"

I started to pace back and forth, thinking hard,

plotting and scheming. It's what Bernie B. does best.

A few minutes later I knew exactly what we had to do.

Chapter 6

BELZER IS THE MAN!

I called Crench into my room. "Where've you been?" I asked.

"Eating candy bars," he said. He held up a Nutty Nutty Bar. He had chocolate smeared all over his face.

"I want you to hear my idea," I said. "It's a brilliant idea."

"Dude, have you ever had any other kind?" Crench said. He sat down next to Feenman on my bed. They were both sitting on Gassy. But the fat, lazy bulldog didn't seem to care.

"Belzer has to win the Heinie Prize," I said. "Most Outstanding Fourth Grader. That will impress his parents, and they'll let him stay here."

"Huh?"

Their mouths dropped open. A wet gob of chocolate fell out of Crench's mouth, onto my white shag rug.

"Belzer? Most Outstanding Fourth Grader?" Feenman cried. "But, Bernie—he's kind of a dim bulb. I mean, when he gets dressed in the morning, he pulls his pants down over his head!"

"Have you ever seen him eat soup?" Crench asked. "Most of it goes up his nose!"

"They don't give the Heinie Prize for nose picking!" Feenman said.

"He sucks his thumb. He sleeps with a *blankie!*" Crench exclaimed. "He picks scabs off his knees and *eats* them!"

"You guys are just jealous," I said. "You know that Belzer is *outstanding!* When his parents learn that he has won the Heinie..."

"But, Bernie—did you forget? YOU want that prize!" Crench said. "If you win, you'll be King of the Campus. It's what you've always wanted."

"Forget about me," I told them. "I don't count. I've gotta take care of my friend Belzer. I always take good care of my guys."

I grabbed the candy bar from Crench's hand. I stuffed it into my mouth and gobbled it up.

"Hey! Why'd you do that?" Crench shouted.

"It's not good for you," I said. *Munch munch.* "See? That's how I take care of you guys! I watch out for your health. But do you appreciate it? No."

"Mrs. Heinie doesn't like Belzer," Feenman said. "She told him he wasn't born. He slithered out from under a rock."

"She told him he has the IQ of an egg," Crench said. "But not as much personality."

"She was *teasing* him," I said. "You know her wonderful sense of humor."

"She doesn't have a sense of humor," Feenman said. "She said that Belzer was lower than the wart on the bottom of her foot."

"Well, we all have room for improvement," I said. "We'll just have to show Mrs. H. the *truth* about Belzer."

"The truth?" Crench asked. "What's the truth?"

"That Belzer is the MAN," I said. "The main DUDE. That Belzer is a genius. A brilliant student. A perfect citizen."

The two of them just stared at me with their mouths hanging open. They didn't know what to say.

I waved them to the door. "Hurry. Go get him," I said. "No. Wait. Let him finish my laundry. *Then* bring him in here!"

Chapter 7

A HIGH FEVER?

An hour later they brought Belzer into my room. He dropped the tall stack of clean clothes on my bed. "I used a fabric softener for your boxer shorts, Bernie," he said. "So they'll be feathery soft the way you like them."

Feenman and Crench started to giggle.

"Shut up," I said. "Can I help it if I have sensitive skin?"

I turned to Belzer and put a hand on his shoulder. "Say good-bye to the old Belzer," I said.

He blinked. "Huh?"

"The new Belzer is born today," I told him. "We're going to keep you here in Rotten School. We're gonna make you Outstanding Student and Outstanding Citizen. You're gonna win the Heinie Prize!"

His mouth dropped open. He burped.

"Are you sure about this, Bernie?" Feenman said.

I closed Belzer's mouth for him. "We'll shape this guy up in no time," I said. I pulled a fat bug from his hair. "The dude is outstanding on the *inside*. We just have to bring the inside *outside*!"

Belzer blinked again. "Turn me inside out? Won't that hurt?"

"We'll start with his clothes," I said. "Belzer, what's this T-shirt you're wearing under your school blazer? Let me see what it says."

I pulled the blazer open and read the T-shirt:

I'M NOT THE ONLY LOSER ON THIS PLANET!

I tossed my hands into the air. "It's hopeless!" I sighed. "Totally hopeless!"

I heard the *click* of shoes in the hall. Mrs. Heinie poked her head into the room. She squinted at me. "What's hopeless, Bernie?" she demanded.

"Uh...trying to keep up with Belzer," I said. "He's so *brilliant* and *outstanding*, the rest of us can't keep up with him. It's hopeless."

"Go lie down, Bernie," Mrs. Heinie said. "I'll get two aspirins for you. You must be running a high fever."

She hurried away.

Feenman and Crench shook their heads. "This isn't going to work," Crench said. "No way Belzer can win that prize."

I pressed my hand over his mouth. "Don't say that," I said. "You know my motto: 'Never Give Up!' Did I give up when we had to paddle that rubber raft over the raging whitewater falls?"

"Bernie, that was a video game," Crench said.

"But I didn't give up!" I exclaimed. "And I'm not giving up on my pal Belzer. He can be outstanding. I know he can."

I turned to Belzer. He was cleaning the front of his LOSER T-shirt, wiping it with both hands. "I just burped up some of my dinner," he said. "I *hate* when that happens!"

Chapter 8

A FLESH-EATING DISEASE

How could I convince Mrs. Heinie that the biggest loser in the fourth grade should win the Most Outstanding prize? This was a tough job, even for Bernie B.

And it was even tougher because Sherman Oaks wanted the Heinie Prize so badly. I knew that Sherman was the only other kid who had a chance.

The next morning, I ran into Mrs. Heinie downstairs in the Rotten House Commons Room. She was holding a bouquet of purple flowers.

"Aren't these lovely?" she gushed, giving them a

big, noisy sniff. "A dozen purple tulips. My favorite!"

"Where did you get them?" I asked.

"Sherman Oaks gave them to me," she said. "He sends me flowers every morning. As a bribe. He's bribing me to give him the Heinie Prize."

I snickered. "Of course it isn't working," I said. "Bribing you—how ridiculous!"

"Yes, it's definitely working," Mrs. H. replied. "I love flowers. Sherman is number one!" She took another big sniff and inhaled an entire tulip.

"Did you say those were purple *tulips*?" I said. "Oh, no! Didn't you hear about Purple Tulip Fever? It's a flesh-eating disease you catch by touching purple tulips. I saw it on TV. It spreads over your entire body and eats your skin away."

"HUH—?" Mrs. Heinie let out a scream. She heaved the flowers into a trash can. "I'd better go wash! Thanks for the warning, Bernie!"

"No problem," I said. I watched her race up the stairs.

Score one for Bernie B. But I still had my hands full. How could Belzer compete with Sherman and his bribes?

That night, I went to work. . . .

Chapter 9

BERNIE
THE SLAVE

That night in my room, I slid my arm around Belzer's shoulders. "A few lessons from Bernie B.," I said, "and you'll be almost as brilliant, outstanding, and awesome as I am!"

Belzer grinned his lopsided grin at me. "I'm ready," he said. He started to pant like a dog.

"We'll start with your wardrobe," I said.

"I don't have a robe," Belzer replied.

"Your clothes," I said. "Let's check out your clothes." I led him into the tiny room across the hall that he shares with Feenman and Crench. The three of them *insisted* on sharing a room so that I could have my own room. They know I need a lot of space for planning and scheming.

Feenman and Crench sleep in a bunk bed. Belzer has a little cot over the air vent.

Feenman and Crench sat down to watch us. Crench picked up a couple of hot dog–shaped balloons and started to let the air out of them slowly. His hobby is making disgusting noises with balloons—and he's very good at it. We have a *bunch* of talented guys in our dorm. Too bad Belzer isn't one of them.

"What's that pile over there?" I asked, pointing.

"My T-shirts," Belzer said.

"You need plain white shirts to go with your school uniform," I said. "Let's see what you have here. . . ." I started sifting through his T-shirts, reading what they said:

PLEASE DON'T HURT ME

I NEED MEDICATION

WELCOME TO THE PLANET LOSER

DON'T BLAME ME—I WAS BORN LIKE THIS

"These are all loser T-shirts," I said.

Belzer squinted at them. "Really? Do you think so?"

"Get rid of them," I ordered. "You have to wear plain white shirts. And always wear your school tie. You have to look *sharp* from now on. And what's that mountain of smelly rags?" I pointed again.

"The rest of my clothes," Belzer said. "After I do *your* laundry, there's no time to do mine."

I stared at the pile. "When's the last time you did your laundry?"

"Never?" Belzer replied.

"Gloves!" I called to Feenman and Crench. "Quick!" I held up my hands. "Glove me."

Feenman pulled a pair of rubber gloves over my hands. Then I bent down and started picking through the smelly, stained shirts and pants.

"WHOA—!" I let out a startled cry as rats and fat, brown bugs came stampeding out from under the pile.

"Ooh, gross!" Feenman cried. He and Crench went running from the room.

The rats and bugs streamed after them into the hall.

"Okay, pick it all up and follow me," I told Belzer.

He scratched his hair. "Where are we going?"

"To the laundry room," I said. "I'm going to do your laundry."

His eyes bulged. "*You* are going to do *my* laundry?"

"I'm your slave now, Belzer," I said. "I'm going to do *everything* for you—until you win the Heinie."

"My slave?" Belzer said, rubbing his chins. "Okay, slave. Go get me a Foamy Root Beer."

"Don't get cute," I said. I brushed away a tangle of fat, brown bugs from one of his sweaters, and we headed to the laundry room.

Chapter 10

MRS. H. HAS A GOOD LAUGH

The laundry room is in the basement of the Student Center. I stepped in and saw two long rows of gleaming, white washers and dryers. Kids from all three dorms do their own laundry here.

Of course, I'd never been *near* the laundry room. But how hard could it be to work the machines? Not hard at all if you're a genius like someone I know—namely *me*.

I pulled on a double layer of rubber gloves. I didn't want to catch any germs from Belzer's clothes. It took only a few minutes to toss the stuff into different machines, soap them up, and get them rolling.

Belzer stood in the doorway, shaking his head and muttering to himself. He couldn't believe that Bernie B. was working for *him*.

But I had no choice. I had to get him cleaned up. *No way* he could be Most Outstanding Fourth Grader with bugs crawling up and down his sleeves.

Time dragged by. I tried to get a poker game going. But there were only two other kids in the laundry room—third graders—and I'd already won all their money.

The washers stopped spinning. I pulled the clean clothes out and stuffed them into dryers. This was a piece of cake.

I tried to picture a *clean* Belzer. But even I don't have that good an imagination!

"Hey, Bernie," Belzer called, glancing all around. "Where's all my underwear?"

"Take it easy, Belzer," I said. "It's in that little dryer over there." I pointed.

"That's not a dryer!" Belzer cried. "It's a microwave oven. For snacks while you wait for your laundry."

"Oh," I said. "Well, guess what? I just microwaved

your underpants. It *has* to be an improvement—right?"

Belzer let out a groan and pulled open the microwave door. Steam poured out. His underpants were soft and stuck together, like a pile of mashed potatoes.

Okay. So no one's perfect.

I saw Wes Updood come in, so I hurried over to say hi. Wes Updood is Sherman Oaks's friend. But that doesn't stop him from being the coolest guy at Rotten School.

He's so totally beyond cool, no one ever knows what he's talking about. And, dude, does Wes know style! Tonight he had his baggy jeans on backward. And he wore a black vest over his bare chest, also backward. It took me a while to tell which way he was going!

"What's up, Wes?" I called.

He nodded. "Chocolate cupcakes, man," he said. "With the cream filling. Heat 'em and eat 'em—know where I'm comin' from?"

"Well ... yeah," I said. "Heat 'em and eat 'em. I know."

"Montreal, man," he said. We touched knuckles. "Montreal, all day long! No way? *Way!*"

"Way," I agreed.

What was he TALKING about??

"It's the new white meat, right?" He giggled. Like that was a funny joke.

Then he started to back up to the door. Or maybe he was going forward. I couldn't tell.

"Montreal, everybody!" he called, waving to me. "Montreal till you drop!"

He vanished out the door. I turned—and let out a shout.

Belzer had his head stuck in a dryer door!

How was that *possible*?

I dove across the room. Grabbed Belzer by the shoulders and started to tug.

But before I could pull him out, who should step up behind us? Five guesses—and they're all Mrs. Heinie.

Her eyes bulged from behind her thick glasses. She pressed her hands to her cheeks. "Bernie—!"

47

she cried. "What on *earth* is happening here?"

I turned away from Belzer and gave her my best, dimpled grin. "Do you see this, Mrs. Heinie?" I said. "Do you see what this brilliant kid is doing?" I slapped Belzer on the back.

Mrs. Heinie squinted harder.

"Belzer is such an outstanding citizen," I said. "He's watching the *inside* of the dryer to make sure it doesn't catch fire."

I wiped a tear from my eye. "What a guy," I said. "He only cares about the safety of others. Genius!"

Mrs. Heinie frowned at me. "Pull him out," she said. "The genius has turned blue. He isn't breathing."

I tugged Belzer out of the dryer. Then I jumped up and down on his chest to get him breathing again.

He picked up his head. His eyes rolled around. "Montreal?" he moaned. He dropped down on the linoleum.

Mrs. Heinie shook her head. "Can the genius stand up?"

"Of course he can," I said. "But he's inspecting the floor for cracks. That's how much he cares about student safety."

Mrs. H. let out a groan. She started to leave, but I chased after her.

"I know you're thinking about Belzer for the Heinie Prize," I said. "And I think you've made a good choice."

We heard a choking sound. We both watched Belzer cough up a sock.

Mrs. Heinie stomped out, laughing at the top of her lungs. "The Heinie Prize for Belzer?" she cried. And then she laughed even harder.

"I put the idea in her head," I said. "That's the first step, Belzer. She's thinking about you now."

"Montreal," he moaned.

I pulled him to his feet. Then I had a brilliant idea.

"Belzer," I said, "stay here and wash all your clothes. Everything you own. Don't leave until everything is clean."

"Everything?" he murmured.

"Everything," I said. "I'm going to help you, Belzer. You'll see!"

I hurried away to find Flora and Fauna, the Peevish twins.

Chapter 11

WHY THE TWINS SCREAMED

I hurried to the girls' dorm to find Flora Peevish and her twin sister, Fauna. They hang out a lot with Sherman Oaks, but I didn't care about that tonight. I was desperate.

I found them in their dorm's Commons Room watching Japanese sumo wrestling on TV with a bunch of other girls. The girls were all jumping up and down on the couches, cheering and shouting.

The Peevish twins are kinda cute. They're short and thin and have straight, brown hair, brown eyes, and tiny, turned-up noses that look like elf noses.

They're identical twins and they share their clothes. The only way to tell them apart is to ask them who they are.

One of them gave me a nice greeting: "Beat it. No boys!"

I pointed to the huge dudes in diapers wrestling on TV. "How can you watch those guys?" I asked.

"We think they're cute," she answered.

"Awesome," I said. "You know Belzer, right? You think he's cute, too?"

She stuck her finger down her throat and gagged herself.

"Is that a yes or a no?" I asked.

"Ucccck," her sister said.

One of the fat wrestlers got slammed hard on his back. The girls all clapped and cheered.

I turned to Fauna. "Be honest. What do you think of Belzer?" I asked.

She groaned. "He's like a piece of something you pull out from between your toes."

"So, you have a crush on him?" I said.

"Uccccck."

On TV, the diaper dudes were falling on each

other. The girls cheered and shrieked.

I pulled the Peevish twins into the hall. "Look. I need your help," I said. "I'm doing a science experiment. For extra credit in Mr. Boring's class."

"I know what it is," Flora said. "It's about the plant and insect life that grow on Belzer's body. Right?"

I pinched her cheek. "I can tell you have a crush on him!" I said. "I can see your eyes light up when I mention his name."

"Sick," she muttered.

"Ucccck," Fauna said.

I was winning them over.

"What's the experiment?" Fauna asked. "Why do you need us?"

"I need you to pretend to have *major* crushes on Belzer," I said.

"I'd rather eat cow plop," Flora said.

"Sign me up for that," Fauna said.

I laughed. "Ha-ha-ha. Belzer *loves* girls with a sense of humor!"

"I'm not joking," Flora said. "Bring me the cow plop. I'll show you."

"It's just *pretend*," I said. "Just *pretend* you both

have a crush on him. It's an experiment. To build up his confidence. To see if it'll make him change."

"No way," Fauna said, turning up her already-turned-up nose. "Not even pretend."

"I sat next to Belzer at the movies," Flora said, "and he picked his nose the entire time."

"He scratched himself, too," her sister added. "Flora, did you forget how he kept scratching himself while he picked his nose?"

"Give the guy a break," I said. "He was nervous sitting with you two. He always gets nervous when he's sitting with the two hottest girls in school."

"I could hear his stomach growling," Fauna said. "It sounded like he had a cat trapped in there. He burped up some of his lunch and then he *ate* it."

"Uccccck," Flora said.

"Double ucccck," Fauna said.

"How about if I bribe you?" I asked.

They stared at me. "What's the bribe?"

"Two six-packs of Foamy Root Beer," I said.

Their eyes lit up. "Two six-packs?" Fauna asked.

I knew they don't drink it. They use it for shampoo because it's so foamy.

"Okay. What do we have to do?" Flora asked.

"Follow me," I said.

"Belzer is in the laundry room. Just go in there and make a big fuss over the guy."

"How long do we have to flirt with him?" Fauna asked.

"Give him fifteen minutes. Can you do it?" I asked.

"Ten minutes," Fauna said.

We settled on twelve.

We followed the path across the Great Lawn to the Student Center. A bright half-moon lit up the sky, and a million stars twinkled down on us.

I knew this would help Belzer a lot. Help build his confidence. And I'd make sure to get word to Mrs. Heinie about how popular Belzer was with the girls—because he was so *outstanding*.

The twins followed me through the back door and down the steps to the laundry room. We walked into the bright lights. And gazed at the two rows of washers and dryers.

And then all three of us gasped. Flora and Fauna

opened their mouths—and let out deafening SCREAMS.

Belzer stood there TOTALLY NAKED.

"Belzer? What are you DOING?" I cried.

He shrugged. "Bernie, you told me to wash ALL my clothes!"

Chapter 12

A BOWLING ACCIDENT

"Feenman, be gentle with that box," I said. "It's filled with photo albums of me. Careful not to wrinkle them."

Feenman groaned under the weight of the huge carton. "Where am I carrying this, Bernie?"

"Into your room," I said. "Crench, careful with that poster of me. The frame is delicate glass."

I watched Crench hoist the poster off my wall. He followed Feenman into the tiny room across the hall.

"Belzer, watch how you handle those boxer

shorts," I said. "I have them neatly folded and arranged by color."

"I don't get it, Big B," Belzer said. "Why are you moving out of your room?"

I put a hand on Belzer's shoulder. "I'm giving my room to *you*, Belzer," I said. "And I'm moving into that tiny closet across the hall with Feenman and Crench."

"But, Bernie—" he started.

"No. Don't thank me," I said. "You know I do *anything* for my friends."

"But, Bernie—"

I clapped him on the back. His bubble gum went flying from his mouth. He bent over, picked it up, and popped it back in.

"You need my room, Belzer," I said. "You need room to be alone."

He blew a fat, pink bubble that burst all over his face. "I do?"

"You need room to think outstanding thoughts," I told him. "Room to practice being outstanding."

He was struggling to unstick the gum from his cheeks. "Yes. Outstanding thoughts," he said.

I turned to the door. "Feenman! Crench! Hurry up with Belzer's stuff," I shouted. "Get it in here. He's in a hurry to start thinking outstanding thoughts."

Belzer raised a pointer finger. "I think I have one, Bernie," he said. "I think I have an outstanding thought! OOPS. I forgot it."

I patted him on the head. "Don't strain yourself, Belzer," I said. "You'll get a headache if you try too hard."

Feenman and Crench were sweating and struggling with some heavy cartons from Belzer's room. "What have you got in this box?" Feenman groaned.

"It's my bowling ball collection," Belzer said.

"Bowling balls?" Crench cried. "Belzer, you don't bowl!"

"I know," Belzer replied. "I just like the way they look."

"He's an art lover!" I exclaimed. "See? I told you he was outstanding!"

Feenman dropped to his knees. "How . . . how many balls in this box?" he moaned.

"About ten," Belzer said.

Crench carried a carton in front of him. He couldn't see where he was going. He tripped over Feenman.

"YIKES!"

The carton tipped over. Bowling balls hit the floor and bounced in all directions. Feenman and Crench hit the floor, too.

"Stop them! STOP them!"

Belzer screamed. "Don't let them escape!"

A ball rolled out into the hall. I jumped over Feenman and Crench and took off after it.

The ball spun rapidly to the stairs. Then it started to bounce down the stairs, picking up speed.

To my horror, I saw a figure slowly climbing the stairs.

"Mrs. Heinie—look out!" I screamed. "LOOK OUT!"

Chapter 13

NOSE WARS

Belzer and I dove down the stairs to help Mrs. Heinie. The bowling ball bounced hard into the pit of her stomach. Her glasses went flying. She doubled over and made a loud OOOOOF sound, just like in the cartoons.

Belzer and I lifted her up by the arms. I brushed off the front of her house smock.

Belzer handed Mrs. H. her glasses. "Hope my bowling ball is okay," he murmured.

"What was THAT?" she gasped, glancing up and down the stairs.

"A brilliant new game that Belzer invented," I said. "It's called Stair Bowling."

She blinked several times. She rubbed her stomach. "Stair Bowling?"

"Yes. Belzer is so clever!" I said. "It's a fabulous, new game. It'll probably make Belzer a million dollars!"

Belzer blushed. "You really think so?"

I stepped in front of him. "He's a total genius, Mrs. H.," I said. "He invents these new games all the time. Have you seen his outstanding, new computer game? It's called Stand Up for Rotten School. Belzer is so loyal! He told me he'd give his *life* for this school!"

Mrs. Heinie stared at Belzer. "He would? That's very interesting. . . . Could he do it *tonight?*"

I was getting to her. I could see her brain whirring. "I know you're thinking of Belzer for the Heinie Prize—and you're right!" I said.

"Did you see the *huge* box of chocolates Sherman sent me this morning?" Mrs. Heinie said. "That boy really knows how to bribe. I'm just about ready to engrave his name on the trophy."

"Belzer doesn't *have* to bribe!" I cried. "Because he's a genius!"

She groaned and rubbed her stomach. "We'll see what a genius he is when he hands in his term paper."

I gulped. "Huh? Term paper?"

"Term paper," she said. "You've heard those words, right?"

"But Belzer is way too brilliant to write a term paper," I said. "He has to think deep thoughts. He has to keep inventing new games."

"Term paper," Mrs. Heinie said. She spelled the words for me.

I watched her hobble up to her apartment in the attic, holding her stomach.

"Term paper," I muttered. "Term paper."

Sherman's bribes were working. He was way ahead of Belzer. Belzer *had* to write the best term paper ever written. But—how?

And then three other words popped into my mind: Billy the Brain.

Chapter 14

BRILLIANT!

Billy the Brain is the smartest kid at Rotten School. He can read a book with one eye closed!

I knew he was the perfect person to write Belzer's term paper for him.

I trotted down the stairs to Billy's room. I found him in the hall. He was holding the runaway bowling ball in his hands, studying it closely.

"Yo, Billy," I said.

"Look what I found," he said. He held up the blue and black ball. "I think it fell through the roof. It's part of an asteroid that must have exploded."

"No—" I started.

"Check out the blue markings in the ancient rock," Billy said. "Many centuries ago, those could have been rivers."

"It's not an asteroid. It's a bowling bowl," I said.

"I knew that!" Billy replied. "I was just testing you."

"How did you do on Mr. Boring's surprise Science quiz?" I asked.

"I aced it," Billy said. "A solid 36."

"Excellent!" I cried. I slapped him a high five. I shouldn't have done it. He dropped the bowling ball on his foot.

Billy started moaning in pain and hopping up and down on one foot. Some guys came out of their rooms and started clapping along.

"Go back in your rooms. He isn't dancing!" I shouted.

They clapped along anyway, until Billy finally stopped hopping. He limped into his room, and I followed him.

He has big, color posters of human brains on his walls. And a red and gold sign that reads: I'M SMARTER THAN YOU.

Well, sure, sometimes he brags a little. But a kid who can read an entire comic book in less than a day has a right to brag!

"I need you to do me a favor," I said. "How long does it take you to write a term paper?"

"About ten minutes," he said. "Unless I'm having a bad day. Then it takes fifteen."

"Can you write a brilliant term paper for Belzer?" I asked.

"No problem," he said. "What is the subject?"

"'The History of the Internet,'" I told him.

Billy rubbed his chin. "Very good subject," he said. "Did you know that before we had computers, people tried to get the Internet on their toasters? But it didn't work. Toast kept popping up, and they couldn't read the screen."

"Well—" I started.

"And back in the day, before we had electricity," Billy said, "kids had to play video games by candle-light!"

I stared at him. What a moron.

"You know what?" I said. "I think I'll write Belzer's term paper myself."

Chapter 15

THE BERNIE SHUFFLE

Two nights later I was busy in my new room. The door swung open, and Feenman and Crench burst in, panting like dogs.

"Bernie—come quick," Feenman said.

"Emergency!" Crench cried. "It's a poker emergency."

I squinted at him. "Excuse me?"

"Sherman is holding a poker game, and he's beating everyone," Crench said, tugging my arm. "Come quick, Bernie. You've got to join the game."

"You've got to do the Bernie Shuffle," Feenman said.

That's my special card trick. As I shuffle the cards, I see every single card in the deck.

"Then you've gotta do the Bernie Deal," Feenman said.

That's when I deal from the bottom, middle, and top of the deck, and no one is the wiser.

"You've gotta take Sherman down," Crench said. "Hurry. I've got the sandpaper to get your fingers nice and dry." He tried to tug me up again.

"Sorry, dudes. Not tonight," I said. "Can't you see I'm busy here?" I pointed to the piles of books and papers on my desk.

"Too busy to teach Sherman a poker lesson?" Feenman cried. "You're joking, right?"

"I'm not joking," I said. "What are you playing for? Money?"

Feenman laughed. "We can't play for money, Bernie. You took all our money—remember? We're playing for chips."

"What kind of chips?" I asked.

"That new garlic and onion flavor," Crench said. "We've got a whole bag."

My favorite! I jumped to my feet and grabbed the

sandpaper from Crench. I started to sand my fingers.

No. Stop, Bernie. No way.

I shook my head. "I'm finishing Belzer's math homework," I said. "Then I have to get back to work on Belzer's term paper."

"But, Big B—" Crench protested.

"Then I have to walk my dog," I said. "And I've got two loads of Belzer's laundry at the laundry room. When I finish that, I have to set out Belzer's clothes for tomorrow. I have to shine his shoes. Then I have to plan what I'm going to bring him for breakfast."

"Bernie, what's happened to you?" Crench cried. "You've become Belzer's *slave!*"

"Worth it," I said. "Worth it, dudes. We don't want Belzer to leave school, do we? Once he wins the Heinie Prize and is King of the Campus, the king will go back to being *my* slave. It's worth it."

They walked out, shaking their heads. I turned back to the math book and continued solving the problems.

I worked all night. "Worth it. Worth it," I kept muttering to myself.

The next morning I stumbled into class, yawning

and rubbing my tired eyes.

I dropped into my seat, planning to take a short nap. But Mrs. Heinie's words snapped me to attention. "I hope you are all ready for the Geography test," she said. "It counts *half* your grade."

Half?

I forgot all about it!

Chapter 16

"WE WEREN'T CHEATING!"

I called out to Mrs. Heinie, "I'm sorry. We can't take a test today," I said.

She squinted at me through her glasses. "And why not?"

"It's a holiday," I said. "I know how you like to celebrate holidays, Mrs. H. We all admire that about you. You're a real *holiday* person."

She let out a groan. "What holiday?"

Think fast, Bernie. Think fast.

"Uh...it's Saint Mort's Day," I said.

She squinted even harder. "Who is Saint Mort?"

"Well…uh…" I could feel beads of sweat rolling down my forehead. I loosened my school tie. "Saint Mort? He's the one who … freed all the moths," I said. "You remember that story, right? How he freed all the moths? We always celebrate it on this day, and—"

"Shut your piehole, Bernie," Mrs. Heinie said kindly. "Everyone take out a sheet of paper and number from one to two hundred."

It was going to be a lonnnnng test.

Especially for me, since I didn't even read the chapters!

She passed out the test booklets, and I glanced at the questions. I knew I didn't know any of the answers.

But does Bernie B. know the meaning of the word *panic*? No way.

I can write my way out of any test.

I lowered my head and started to write. I put down as much information as I knew. I even wrote a paragraph about Saint Mort and the moths.

I wrote until my hand was sweating. I stopped to wipe it off on my blazer sleeve. And that's when I saw Sherman—copying my answers!

I looked down again. I pretended I didn't see him. But I did. I glanced over at him.

Yes. His eyes were on my paper. He read my answers, then copied them word for word onto his own paper.

Imagine that! Sherman Oaks copying off me. He probably forgot to buy the answers from someone.

He was being very sneaky about it, too. Coughing into his hand as he read my paper. Pretending to sneeze while he read my answers.

I decided to have some fun with him.

I wrote:

"Mount McKinley is actually a very large, very tall person—not a mountain."

I glanced over and saw Sherman write it down on his paper.

Then I wrote:

"Santa Claus lives at the North Pole with all his elves."

Sherman wrote that down, too.

This was fun. Giggling to myself, I wrote:

"I'm a total jerk."

I followed Sherman's pencil as he wrote: "I'm a total jerk."

I couldn't help it. I burst out laughing. I gazed at Sherman's paper. "Dude, you have such perfect handwriting," I whispered.

"Of course I do," Sherman whispered back. "If you want to be outstanding, you have to have perfect handwriting."

I heard a book slam at the front of the room. "Bernie! Sherman!" Mrs. Heinie shouted. "Come see me, please."

Everyone in class turned to stare at us.

"You're both out of here. I saw you cheating!" Mrs. Heinie said, pointing at us.

"But—but—" Sherman sputtered. "We weren't cheating. He was just admiring my handwriting!"

Mrs. H. rolled her eyes. "That's the worst excuse I ever heard."

She motioned to the door. "Out of here. Both of you. And . . . you realize, I hope, that you are *both* out of the running for the Heinie Prize. Fuhgedaboutit!"

Sherman gasped. "But I already have the display

case!" He reached into his pocket and pulled out a hundred-dollar bill. He shoved it at Mrs. Heinie. "Will this help change your mind?"

"Out! Both of you! Out!" Mrs. Heinie shouted.

Sherman was shaking his head, muttering to himself. "She always liked my bribes. She told me I was going to win." He was totally upset.

But I had a grin on my face. Why?

Because I'm a GENIUS! That's why.

Don't you see? With Sherman out, Belzer actually stood a chance of winning the prize.

Now I needed an idea. A *big* idea to make absolutely sure Belzer won.

And the idea came to me as I was walking past Pooper's Pond. I held my nose to keep out the smell of the muddy water. And as I started to cross the little bridge over the pond, the idea struck me:

If Belzer saves my life, he'll HAVE to be Most Outstanding Citizen!

Chapter 17

MOONLIGHT OVER POOPER'S POND

That night I dragged Belzer to Pooper's Pond. It was a bright, clear night. The smelly water of the small pond shimmered like silver in the moonlight.

I pulled Belzer to the little stone bridge. "Here we are," I said. "Are you ready to be a hero?"

Belzer stared at me. "Huh?"

"Listen to me," I said. I gripped his chin and held his face pointed at me. It's the only way to keep his attention.

"Mrs. Heinie takes a walk around campus every night," I told him. "She's going to pass this bridge in exactly twelve-and-a-half minutes."

Belzer raised a hand to check his watch. But he wasn't wearing a watch. He studied his wrist.

I gripped him by the chin again. "Are you listening? Here's the plan. I'm going to pretend to fall off this bridge. I fall into the pond. I thrash around. I'm drowning. You jump in. You pull me out."

"I do?" Belzer said. He couldn't talk too well. I was gripping his chin too hard.

"Mrs. Heinie sees you save my life," I said, "and you're a hero. She *has* to give you the Heinie Prize."

Belzer pulled his chin free. "But, Bernie," he said, "the pond is two feet deep."

"It doesn't matter," I said. "She'll see me in trouble down there. I'll be flapping around, screaming for help. You'll be a hero, Belzer. You'll be *outstanding*!"

Belzer shook his head. "I...can't do it, Big B."

"Excuse me? Why not?"

"I'm afraid of water," Belzer said.

"It's only two feet deep," I said.

"It doesn't matter," Belzer replied. "Really. Holding a glass of water makes me seasick!"

I checked my watch. There wasn't time to argue.

Mrs. H. would be at the bridge in exactly ten-and-three-quarter minutes.

"Belzer, you don't want to leave Rotten School, do you?"

He shook his head.

"Then you've got to be outstanding. You've got to save my life."

He lowered his head. "I ... I just can't, Bernie," he said.

Suddenly, I had an idea. "Wait right here," I said. "Can you do that?"

"If I don't look down at the water," Belzer said.

"Don't move," I ordered. "I'll be right back.

I raced to the dorm. I knew what I had to do to make Belzer a hero.

A few minutes later, I came running back to the little bridge. What was I carrying? Two of Belzer's precious bowling balls.

Did you forget that Bernie B. is a genius?

I saw Mrs. Heinie walking toward the pond. Right on time. I raced onto the bridge. I raised the bowling balls high so that Belzer could see them. And then I JUMPED into the water.

The bowling balls and I made
a loud splash.

I heard Mrs. Heinie gasp.
She saw me go in.

And then I heard Belzer's
horrified scream: "No!
No! Not my beautiful
bowling balls!"

And he dove in
after them.

Chapter 18

BELZER
THE HERO

A few seconds later I was sprawled on my back on the grass. Belzer stood next to me, wiping the two bowling balls dry with his T-shirt.

I spit some water from my mouth and grinned up at Mrs. Heinie. "Did you see that?" I said.

"I saw it, but I don't believe it," Mrs. H. replied.

"I was taking the bowling balls to the wood shop to polish them," I explained. "I lost my balance and fell into the pond."

I raised my head and pointed to Belzer. "Did you see how that HERO dove into the water? He pulled me out and saved my life."

Mrs. Heinie frowned at me. "It looked to me like YOU had to pull Belzer out."

I jumped up and swiped off her eyeglasses. "Have you checked these lately? They look kinda weak to me."

I handed them back to her. "Belzer was a *super-hero*!" I said. "I...I was going under for the *third time*! He saved my life."

Mrs. H. squinted at Belzer for the longest time. "He's a hero? Are you *sure*?"

Belzer burped up some pond water.

"An outstanding citizen if I ever saw one!" I said.

"Hmmmm," Mrs. Heinie replied. "Hmmmmm."

What's the next chapter in this suspenseful drama? It's the Award Ceremony.

Did I do it? Did I rescue my slave—er, I mean, my *friend*? Did I turn Belzer into a winner?

The suspense is *killing* me....

Chapter 19

A SURPRISE WINNER

Every fourth grader at Rotten School trooped into the gym for the big Award Ceremony. Mrs. Heinie stood under the scoreboard with Headmaster Upchuck at her side. We all sat down on the floor, facing them.

The Headmaster is very short. He came up to Mrs. Heinie's knees.

She lifted him onto a box so that he could speak into the microphone. "Is this on?" he asked. His voice boomed over the gym, echoing off the tile walls.

Feenman, Crench, and I squeezed up near the front. We all had our fingers crossed.

Was I nervous? Does a monkey have bad breath? Of *course* I was nervous. I'd slaved long and hard for this moment.

"Feenman, wake Belzer up," I said. "This could be his big moment."

Feenman grabbed Belzer's shoulders and shook him awake.

"Is this on?" Headmaster Upchuck repeated. He tapped the microphone several times. It sounded like drumbeats echoing over the gym. Lots of kids held their ears.

Sherman Oaks dropped down beside me. He had a grin on his face. He pushed a silver trophy toward me.

"What's that? The Dork of the Month Award?" I asked. "Why don't you give someone *else* a chance to win that?"

"It's my own personal trophy," Sherman said. "For 'Best Handwriting.' My parents sent it to me because they still believe I'm outstanding. It's solid silver. It cost two thousand dollars."

I studied it. I read the name engraved in big letters on the side: HERMAN.

"They misspelled your name," I said.

"We're not a close family," Sherman replied.

"Is this on?" Headmaster Upchuck asked again.

"YESSSSS!" everyone screamed.

"You're all Rotten students," he announced. "But only one fourth grader can be outstanding enough to win the Heinie Prize. Mrs. Heinie has picked the winner. The rest of you are all losers. But I mean that in the nicest way."

He climbed down off the box and backed away.

Mrs. Heinie stepped up to the microphone and cleared her throat several times. "I give this prize every year to the Most Outstanding Student and Most Outstanding Citizen," she said.

I felt my throat tighten. My hands were sweating. My heart was pounding. This was the big moment I'd been waiting for.

"Feenman, wake up Belzer again," I said.

He shook Belzer awake.

"This year," Mrs. Heinie continued, "the fourth grade class was truly rotten in every way. I thought about not giving any prize at all. But I guess I have to. So … the winner is …"

I held my breath. I shut my eyes.

"BELZER!" Mrs. Heinie announced.

Huh? Did she really say Belzer?

Yes!

All us Rotten House guys jumped to our feet. We clapped and shouted and pumped our fists in the air. We slapped high fives and low fives and did the secret Rotten House Handshake.

Then I shoved Belzer to the front of the gym.

"Congratulations, Belzer," Mrs. Heinie said, shaking his hand. "Now that you're standing in front of the whole school, would you like to tell us your *first* name?"

Belzer blinked at her. "I don't know it," he said. "My parents never told it to me."

"Well, congratulations, anyway," she said. She turned to the Headmaster. "Mr. Upchuck, would you like to shake Belzer's hand?"

"No thanks," he replied.

Mrs. Heinie handed Belzer a big, silver trophy. She placed a silver crown on his head. "You are now

King of the Campus!" she announced. She shook his hand again.

"Uh ... thanks," Belzer said. A terrific thank-you speech.

Kids gave one last cheer. Then they stood up and started to walk out of the gym.

I hurried over to the newly crowned king and slapped him on the back. "We did it!" I cried. "All my hard work and slaving for you paid off big-time. You don't have to thank me, Belzer. I know I deserve it. But I don't want your thanks. I'm just happy to see that *outstanding* smile on your face!"

Belzer straightened his crown. Then he gave me a shove toward the door. "Bernie, go get me a root beer," he said.

Uh-oh.

Chapter 20

THE KING SPEAKS

Feenman, Crench, and I hurried back to Rotten House. We were feeling good. We saw Sherman trying to show off his loser trophy to April-May June and some other girls. But they weren't interested.

Belzer was king, thanks to Bernie B.

"How do I do it, dudes?" I asked my friends. We slapped knuckles again. "How do I do it?"

"Pure genius?" Feenman asked.

I nodded. "You got *that* right!"

"Now Belzer won't have to leave school," Crench said. "He can go back to waiting on you hand and foot."

"You got *that* right!" I said again.

We marched into our little room. I picked up the letter from Belzer's parents. "Say good-bye to this!" I said.

I raised the letter high. I started to rip it in two and throw it away. But I stopped.

"Whoa, dudes!"

I stared at the handwriting.

The beautiful, perfect handwriting.

"Where did I see this?" I asked my friends. "I just saw this handwriting somewhere."

And then I let out a hoarse cry. "It's SHERMAN'S!" I screamed. "SHERMAN wrote the letter! Belzer's parents DIDN'T WRITE IT!"

I took several deep breaths. I wanted to scream and scream. But Bernie B. never loses control.

A trick. A vicious prank. The letter was a fake—an evil prank that ruined my life for *days!*

Feenman studied the letter. "Sherman got you good *this* time," he said. "What are you going to do?"

"I don't know," I said. "I have to think about it when I'm calmer. I—"

Belzer burst into the room, wearing his crown.

He pushed a white shirt into my face. "Bernie," he said, "this shirt you washed for me. Look at it. You didn't get the stain out. Go wash it again."

I shoved it away. "Huh? Remember, Belzer? You burped up potato salad all down the front? That stain won't come out."

He pushed the shirt back in my face.

"Try again," he said.

I tossed the shirt on the floor. "Forget the shirt," I said. "It's time to move my stuff back into my room."

Belzer stared at me. "You're joking, right?" he sneered. "It's *my* room now, Bernie. The King of the Campus doesn't share a room. That's the king's room. So stay out!"

The king stomped into his room.

The three of us whimpered in shock. "Who *was* that?"

We didn't have time to think about it. A few seconds later, Belzer drop-kicked my fat bulldog, Gassy, into our room. "Keep that stink bomb away from the king!" he shouted.

"But … but …," I sputtered. "Belzer, it's time for you to take him for his four o'clock walk."

"I don't walk animals," Belzer said, his fat nose in the air. "I have to stay in my room and think outstanding thoughts."

He slammed the door in my face.

I turned to Feenman and Crench. "He'll get over it," I said. "In a few hours he'll remember he's an idiot."

They both shook their heads. Crench put his hand on my shoulder. "Bernie," he said softly, "you've created a MONSTER!"

Chapter 21

THE MONSTER STRIKES!

Crench never spoke truer words.

The next morning I was talking to April-May June on our way to class. April-May is my girlfriend, only she doesn't know it yet. In fact, she barely speaks to me.

"April-May, would you like to watch the eclipse of the moon with me tonight?" I asked.

She stared at me with those stunning blue eyes. "There *is* no eclipse tonight," she said.

"I know," I said. "But we could wait for one."

Suddenly, Belzer appeared. He tugged April-May

away. "The king doesn't want you talking to his girl-friend," he barked.

I laughed. "Excuse me? Girlfriend? You're joking, right?"

April-May shrugged. "Well, face it, Bernie. Belzer *is* the most outstanding kid on campus." She walked off arm in arm with him.

I couldn't believe it. April-May and Belzer?

I followed them across the lawn. We came to Wes Updood. He was sitting under a tree, practicing his saxophone.

Belzer stuck his fist in the sax's horn. "Do you have a permit?" he asked Wes. "You need a music permit from the King of the Campus if you want to play outdoors."

Wes couldn't believe it. He had to give Belzer five dollars for a music permit.

Belzer shoved the money into his pocket. "If you see any other musicians," he said to Wes, "tell 'em to pay up. If you wanna swing, you pay the king!"

I couldn't stand it. I ran to find Feenman and Crench.

"Where were you guys?" I asked. "I couldn't find you this morning."

Crench shook his head. "We had to go see Headmaster Upchuck," he said. "We didn't make our beds this morning. And Belzer *snitched* on us."

"Belzer says all dorm rules must be followed," Feenman told me. "He says the king must enforce every single rule."

I slapped my forehead. "What am I going to do? King Belzer is out of control!"

Across the lawn, I saw Sherman Oaks standing next to a pile of trash. I ran over to him. "How could you write that phony letter?" I asked angrily. "Do you know what you've done?"

"It was a joke," Sherman said. "I was just trying to shake things up."

"Well, you shook things up," I snarled.

Sherman sighed. "Tell me about it. In the Dining Hall last night, Belzer grabbed the last slice of pizza off my tray. He said the king gets all the pizza he wants."

"Nice," I said, rolling my eyes.

"After dinner Belzer climbed on my three-thousand-dollar bike," Sherman moaned. "You know. The one with the gold handlebars. And he rode away."

"But Belzer doesn't know how to ride a bike," I said.

"Tell me about it," Sherman said again. "See that heap of trash over there? That's my bike!"

I stared at the twisted, mangled mess. "He totaled it," I muttered.

"Everyone hates Belzer now,"

Sherman said. "He snitches on kids. And he makes them buy five-dollar permits for just about everything. I had to buy a comb permit to comb my perfect, blond hair this morning."

"We have to stop him," I said.

Sherman stared at me. "How?"

"You and I have to w-w-w-w…" I couldn't get the words out. Too painful. I couldn't say them.

I took a deep breath and started again.

"We have to w-w-w … we have to WORK TO-GETHER!"

Chapter 22

A PALACE FOR THE KING

Sherman and I walked back and forth across the Great Lawn, hatching a plan. It was a nasty, evil plan. But we both agreed that Belzer deserved it.

That afternoon Belzer returned to Rotten House to find his room cleaned out. Totally empty.

"Hey—!" He scratched his red hair. "Bernie, I told you—this is the king's room now. Bring back my stuff."

"Not my idea," I said. "Sherman cleaned out your room."

"Huh? Sherman? Why?" He scratched his hair more.

Sherman appeared, just as we'd planned. "The king can't live in a shabby pit like Rotten House," he told Belzer. "All this dirt and dust and clutter? Guys playing tackle football in the hall? Loud music?"

Sherman put his arm around Belzer's shoulders. "Come with me, King Belzer. You have to room at Nyce House, where it's clean and quiet. And you can live like a king!"

Belzer took one last glance at his room. "You're right," he said. "This place *is* a pit. I don't belong here."

Sherman grinned at him. "You and I are going to be good buddies. I know how to treat a king the way he deserves!"

As he led Belzer away, Sherman turned and flashed me a thumbs-up.

So far, so good.

Chapter 23

KING BELZER SUFFERS

The next morning I crept out of Rotten House at dawn. I never get up before the sun. The darkness makes my skin itch. But I knew today it was going to be worth it.

I sneaked across the silent, empty campus to the back of Nyce House and climbed in through an open window. I knew where to find Belzer. In the Commons Room, with Sherman and a bunch of other guys.

I moved silently down the hall. Yes! There they were. Sherman had the list in his hand. The list of activities we had dreamed up for King Belzer.

I hunched down in the doorway and watched.

Activity One: Exercise Workout at Dawn. Poor Belzer. He started to sweat after one deep knee bend. Sherman worked him hard. Push-ups, sit-ups, jumping jacks, and things I don't know the names of. Painful. Painful.

After about ten minutes, Belzer flopped around on the floor, going *urk urk* like a seal. Three guys had to carry him into the meeting room.

Activity Two: Quizzing One Another on Topics from the Newspaper. I had to giggle. King Belzer didn't know *anything*. "Let's discuss our leader's speech last night," Sherman said.

Belzer stared at him. "Our leader? You mean SpongeBob?"

"SpongeBob isn't our leader," Joe Sweety told Belzer. "SpongeBob isn't real."

Belzer's mouth dropped open. "He *isn't*?"

The guys kept on asking him questions about the news. Belzer pretended to have a coughing fit.

Next activity for King Belzer: Singing in a Barbershop Quartet. It was totally gross. I covered my ears.

Next on the list: Sherman made all the guys read from the U.S. Constitution out loud. Belzer had trouble sounding out the words. He muttered to himself, totally embarrassed.

Then Sherman brought in a carton of accordions, and they took accordion lessons for an hour. Belzer pulled too hard and ripped his accordion in half.

"Can we stop now?" he begged, his whole body shaking. "Are we done?"

"Just starting, dude," Sherman said, grinning. "You're one of us now. This is what we do every morning."

Next came posture lessons. Then, Fun with Algebra Equations. Then choir practice. Then origami. Belzer couldn't get the hang of origami. After a few minutes, his hands were covered in paper cuts.

Belzer looked like a dried-up SpongeBob, and it was only eight o'clock! According to the list Sherman and I had dreamed up, Belzer had two more hours of wonderful Nyce House activities.

I sneaked back outside. I couldn't help it. I opened my mouth and shouted out a loud victory whoop. I cheered myself all the way back to the dorm.

I found Feenman and Crench carrying my stuff back into my room. Crench carried my desk on his back. He was grunting and groaning.

"You're gonna miss Belzer," he groaned. "Who else is going to bring you breakfast in bed, dress you, walk your dog, and carry you piggyback to class?"

"Don't worry about Belzer," I said. "He'll be back."

I checked my watch. "Synchronize your watches, dudes," I said. "Belzer will be back here by noon."

They checked their watches.

"Now, get moving," I said. "Bring my bed back in here. Careful with the mattress. It's a pillow-top. Don't wrinkle it!"

Chapter 24

11:59

At 11:59 that morning, Feenman, Crench, and I sat in my room, waiting. Listening.

"How do you know he'll be here in one minute?" Crench asked.

"Ssshhh. Do you hear something?" I whispered.

We listened harder.

Yes. I heard the creak of heavy footsteps on the stairs. Someone was wheezing and panting as he climbed.

Belzer staggered into the room.

I checked my watch. Noon.

Hey, I never miss.

Belzer stood hunched over in the doorway, sweating, shaking, panting. His freckles were quivering on his face.

No one said a word. I waited for him to start begging.

"Bernie, please . . . ," he started. "Can I come back?"

"Come back *here?*" I said. "Why, King Belzer, you wouldn't want to live in a pit like this!"

"Please, Bernie—I can't take it in Nyce House. This morning we had to learn how to KNIT. Then we all sang 'Row, Row, Row Your Boat' as a round—for hours! Then we planted herbs in an herb garden. Then we all had to dig into our wallets and give money to CHARITY. It's SICK! Totally SICK over there!"

"Sounds like a lot of good fun," I said. "It's so boring here at Rotten House."

"Please, Bernie"—Belzer grabbed the front of my shirt and tugged it—"please, please, please. Let me come back."

"I don't think so," I said. "Remember, you're the

King of the Campus. You have to live in style."

"Forget the king stuff," Belzer said. "I just want to go back to the way it was."

I studied him. "You think you could?"

"Yes, yes, oh yes!" he cried. "I'll walk Gassy. I'll do your laundry. I'll do your homework. I'll carry you piggyback to class every morning."

I stared at him. I rubbed my chin as if I were thinking about it, thinking hard. I shook my head a few times.

Finally, I said, "Okay, Belzer. You can come back. You can move back into the little closet with Feenman and Crench!"

"Oh, thank you, Bernie!" he cried. He had tears running down his face. "Thank you! Thank you! You won't be sorry."

"Okay," I said. "Glad that's settled. Glad being king didn't spoil you, Belzer. Glad you're back to your old self. Now you can go get me a root beer."

"Get your own root beer," he said.

ROTTEN SCHOOL

THE NYCE HOUSE GHOST

Later I closed the door to my room. I paced back and forth for hours, planning and plotting. Then I did some plotting and planning.

Nobody can plan and plot and plot and plan like Bernie B.

Finally, I had the perfect idea. I was going to make Joe Sweety think there was a ghost in Nyce House, his dorm. And that it was after HIM!

Could I do it? Does a salmon have a nose?

I needed Feenman for the first part of my plan. I told him exactly what to say. Then I took him to the gym.

Joe Sweety lifts weights in the gym every morning before classes. Sometimes when the gym is locked, Joe lifts Coach Bunz's car instead.

Sure enough, there was The Big Sweety, huffing and puffing in the center of the floor. He was only lifting 200-pound weights this morning. Guess he wanted to take it easy.

I pulled Feenman close to him. I wanted to make sure Joe heard everything we said. "He's listening," I whispered to Feenman. "Remember, repeat everything I told you."

Then I started to talk very loudly. "The Nyce House ghost is a hundred years old. He returns every five years," I said. "And he always goes after guys named Joe."

I glanced behind me. That *definitely* caught Joe's attention.

"Why only guys named Joe?" Feenman asked.

"A hundred years ago, a big dude named Joe used to sit on him and tickle him till he peed. Soon the poor guy died of embarrassment. From then on, he hated anyone named Joe. Every five years he returns to Nyce House to haunt *another* Joe!"

I heard a loud THUD. The floor shook. Sweety had dropped the weights on his foot.

He hopped over to me on his other foot and grabbed me by the shoulder. "You're joking about that ghost—right? Tell me you're joking."

"Oh. Sorry," I said. "I didn't know you were listening. Don't pay any attention. Just because *everyone* is talking about it doesn't mean it's true."

"Don't worry about it," Feenman added. "The ghost only comes once every five years."

"How many years has it been?" Joe asked.

I pretended to count on my fingers. "Uh...five," I said. "But don't worry about it, Joe. The ghost only comes in months with the letter *R* in them."

Sweety went pale. "But *this* month has an *R* in it!" he cried. He grabbed the front of my shirt. "Listen, how can you tell if it's haunting *you?*"

"Don't worry about it," I said. "Do you still weigh yourself every morning to make sure you're the biggest, meanest fourth grader?"

"Yeah. Of course," Sweety replied.

"Well," I said, "you can tell if the ghost is after you. It uses its spirit powers to make you lose weight."

Sweety's mouth dropped open. "Huh? Lose weight?"

"That's the first sign," I said.

"Don't worry about it," Feenman said. "The ghost only goes after Joes who are left-handed."

"But . . . but . . ." Sweety sputtered. "I'M left-handed!"

"Don't even *think* about it," I said. "It's just a dumb legend. Forget we even mentioned it."

Sweety nodded. His chin was trembling. He turned and hopped out of the gym on his good foot.

Feenman and I laughed. We touched knuckles and did the secret Rotten House Handshake.

"Did you see the look on his face?" Feenman said. "He's terrified."

"Call that terrified?" I said. "Bernie B. hasn't even *started* yet!"

ABOUT THE AUTHOR

R.L. Stine graduated from Rotten School with a solid D+ average, which put him at the top of his class. He says that his favorite activities at school were Scratching Body Parts and Making Armpit Noises.

In sixth grade, R.L. won the school Athletic Award for his performance in the Wedgie Championships. Unfortunately, after the tournament, his underpants had to be surgically removed.

After graduation, R.L. became well known for writing scary book series such as The Nightmare Room, Fear Street, Goosebumps, and Mostly Ghostly, and a short story collection called *Beware!*

Today, R.L. lives in New York City, where he is busy writing stories about his school days.

For more information about R.L. Stine,
go to www.rottenschool.com
and www.rlstine.com